THE GOBBLE DEGOOK BOOK

This edition first published in 2019 by Gecko Press
PO Box 9335, Wellington 6141, New Zealand
info@geckopress.com

Text © Joy Cowley 2019
Illustrations © Giselle Clarkson 2019
Edition © Gecko Press Ltd 2019

"Nicketty-Nacketty Noo-Noo-Noo" is reproduced by permission of Scholastic New Zealand Ltd.

"The Tiny Woman's Coat" and "The Giant Pumpkin" are reproduced by permission of Wendy Pye Publishing Ltd.

First published by Ashton Scholastic Ltd: "Cheese Trap" 1995
First published by Mallinson Rendel in *Pawprints in the Butter* 1991:
"Mean Cat", "Robber Cat", "Long-tail Cat", "Brave Cat", "Garden Cat"
First published by Murdoch Books: "Do Not Drop Your Jellybeans" 1997
First published by Scholastic NZ Ltd: "Duck Walk" 2002,
"The Little Tractor" 2004, and in *Elephant Rhymes* 1997: "SuperJumble", "The Circus"
First published in the *School Journal*: "Goggly Gookers" 1984, "Uncle Andy's Singlet" 2003
First published by School Publications Branch, Department of Education, New Zealand: "Greedy Cat" 1983
First published by Shortland Publications (as "The Lucky Feather"): "Faster Faster" 1986, "The Jumbaroo" 1993
First published by Wright Group in *Tiddalik* 1998: "Nobody Knows"

Gecko Press acknowledges the generous support of Creative New Zealand

Design and typesetting by Vida Kelly
Printed in China by Everbest Printing Co. Ltd, an accredited ISO 14001 & FSC-certified printer

ISBN hardback: 978-1-776572-58-8

For more curiously good books, visit geckopress.com

A Joy Cowley Anthology

THE GOBBLEDEGOOK BOOK

Illustrated by Giselle Clarkson

GECKO PRESS

CONTENTS

THE TINY WOMAN'S COAT

The tiny woman wanted a coat.
"Where will I get the cloth?"
"Try some of our leaves,"
said the autumn trees.
Rustle, rustle, rustle.

The tiny woman wanted a coat.
"Where will I get a needle?"
"Have one of mine,"
said the porcupine.
Sharp, sharp, sharp.

The tiny woman wanted a coat.
"Where will I get some thread?"
"My mane of course,"
said the friendly horse.
Stitch, stitch, stitch.

The tiny woman made her coat
and went out into the storm.
She stayed as snug as a bug in a rug
with her coat to keep her warm.

DUCK

Ducks swim, paddle, paddle.
Ducks talk, quack, quack.
Ducks walk, waddle, waddle,
little duckling at the back.

Little duckling stops to nibble
in the river reeds;
sees a beetle, wriggle, wriggle,
on some water weeds.

WALK

Duckling hunts the beetle,
then a bumblebee,
then an orange butterfly
in a lilac tree.

Little duckling waddles
by the back door mat.
Up jumps furry trouble,
the old scratchy cat!

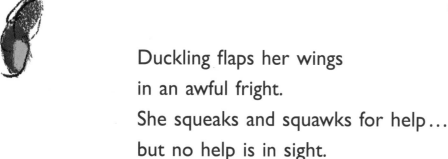

Duckling flaps her wings
in an awful fright.
She squeaks and squawks for help...
but no help is in sight.

The scratchy cat gets closer,
as little duckling squeaks...

and squeaks
and squeaks!

Then

whoosh!

Along come the big ducks,
the angry storm of big ducks,
flapping, flying big ducks,
with snapping, quacking beaks.

A fuss of fur and feathers
and the scratchy cat takes flight.
The little duckling snuggles
in a warm place out of sight.

Big ducks tell the baby
she must not go away.
All kinds of danger
meet little ducks that stray.

Ducks walk, waddle, waddle,
Ducks talk, quack, quack.

Duckling in the middle,
warm in the middle,
safe in the middle…

and not at the back.

NICKETTY-NACKETTY, NOO-NOO-NOO

There once was an ogre called Gobbler Magoo
who lived in a swamp where the wild weeds grew.
Nicketty-nacketty, noo-noo-noo.

A wee wishy woman in an apron of blue,
with her pots and her kettle, was travelling through.
Nicketty-nacketty, noo-noo-noo.

The ogre jumped out and yelled, "Who are you?"
She said, "I'm the maker of good tasty stew."
Nicketty-nacketty, noo-noo-noo.

The ogre then grabbed her and bellowed, "You'll do!
You'll stay here forever and cook me good stew."
Nicketty-nacketty, noo-noo-noo.

He took the wee woman, and all her pots too,
to his mouldy old kitchen to make him some stew.
Nicketty-nacketty, noo-noo-noo.

She sliced and she chopped for a moment or two,
then she filled up a pot with a good tasty brew.
Nicketty-nacketty, noo-noo-noo.

"Hurry! I'm hungry!" cried Gobbler Magoo.
The wee woman smiled and tapped her wee shoe.
Nicketty-nacketty, noo-noo-noo.

At last all the cooking and stirring was through.
The ogre sat down with his pot full of stew.
Nicketty-nacketty, noo-noo-noo.

He ate with a spoon and his five fingers too,
while the wee woman watched him shovel and chew.
Nicketty-nacketty, noo-noo-noo.

Then the chewing got slow and the ogre cried, "Oo!
My teeth seem to stick to this good tasty stew!"
Nicketty-nacketty, noo-noo-noo.

The wee woman laughed and said, "That is true.
The stew's thick and tasty…I cooked it in glue!"
Nicketty-nacketty, noo-noo-noo.

"Mmmm!" mumbled the ogre but he couldn't undo
his hands from the pot or his lips from the stew.
Nicketty-nacketty, noo-noo-noo.

Then the wee wishy woman in her apron of blue
packed her pots and her kettle and said, "Adieu!"
to the stuck-up old ogre who was all in a stew.
Nicketty-nacketty, noo-noo-noo.

Maybe we'll see her as she passes through
with her pots and her pans and her kettle of glue.
(But I don't want to eat her stew. Do you?)

Nicketty-nacketty, noo-noo-noo.

MEAN CAT

Some cats are as fat as cushions.
My cat is long and lean.
Some cats have smiling faces.
My cat's face is mean.
Some cats have names like Tiddles,
Fluff or Butter-paws,
Ginger, Snow or Sweetie.
My cat's name is Jaws.
Some cats eat chunky cat food.
Some think that milk is nice.
My cat eats dead blowflies
and chews the heads off mice.
Some cats play games with paper,
and roll across the floor.
When my cat wants some fun,
it bites the dog next door.

ROBBER CAT

Sly old robber Fattyface
has magnets on her paws
for opening kitchen cupboards
and refrigerator doors.
She robs a house, then vanishes.
All the owner sees
are pawprints in the butter
and toothmarks in the cheese.

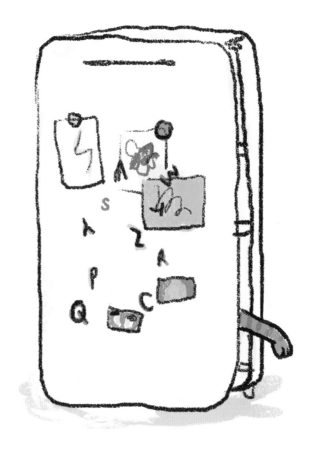

LONG-TAIL CAT

Jake had a long long tail
like the handle of a broom.
Jake slept beside the fire,
his tail across the room.

A kitten saw the tail
and thought it was a snake.
She pounced on it and bit it
and found the snake was Jake!

GARDEN CAT

Beware of the jungle in the garden.
A cat is lurking there.
Between the tomatoes and the rhubarb,
she's made herself a lair.
Feel pity for the garden rat
who wanders out and sees
unblinking eyes and needle teeth
behind the row of peas.

BRAVE CAT

Mother cat goes hunting.
The kittens make a fuss.
"Do be careful, Mother.
Hunting is dangerous!"
"I'm very brave," says Mother.
"I know how to fight.
I'll attack with tooth and claw
and you will eat tonight."
Mother comes home from hunting
when the moon is nearly set.
The kittens run to meet her.
"Oh Mother! What did you get?"
"I've had a terrible battle,"
she laughingly replies.
"Look! I've killed six sausages
and two whole chicken pies!"

THE GIANT PUMPKIN

Mr and Mrs Pip had a giant pumpkin in their garden.

"It's too big to eat," said Mrs Pip. "Let's make it into a cradle for the baby."

"What a good idea!" said Mr Pip.

The pumpkin
grew and grew.

"This pumpkin's too big for a cradle," said Mr Pip. "Let's make it into a bath."

"That's what we'll do," said Mrs Pip.

The pumpkin grew so big that it filled the garden.

"It's far too big for a bath," said Mrs Pip. "But it would make a good double bed."

"So it would," said Mr Pip.

The pumpkin
got bigger.

It squashed the garden fence.

"Too big for a double bed," said Mr Pip. "But if I get some wheels and a motor, it would make a fine truck."

"Of course!" said Mrs Pip.

A week went by.

Now, the pumpkin filled the back yard.

"It's far too big for a truck," said Mrs Pip. "But wouldn't it make a nice house?"

"That's it!" said Mr Pip. "A house!"

But the pumpkin had grown too big.

Suddenly, it
exploded.

The street was filled with bits of pumpkin.

Mr Pip thought for a long time.

"I know what we can do with the pumpkin," he said. "We can make some pumpkin soup. We can have a pumpkin soup party."

"That's just what I was thinking," said Mrs Pip.

And they had a
pumpkin soup party
which lasted a week.

GOGGGLY

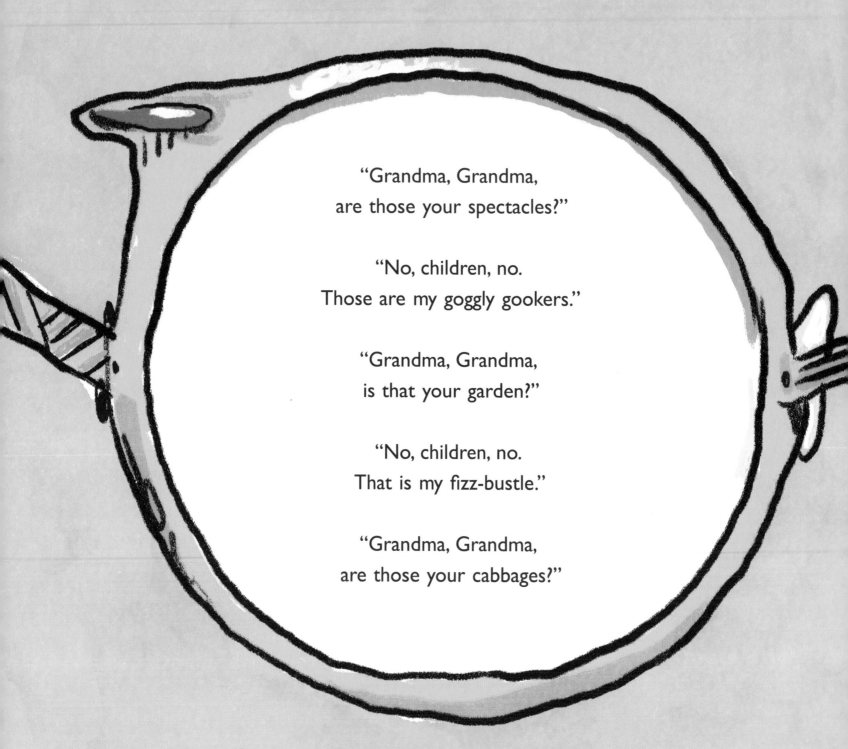

"Grandma, Grandma,
are those your spectacles?"

"No, children, no.
Those are my goggly gookers."

"Grandma, Grandma,
is that your garden?"

"No, children, no.
That is my fizz-bustle."

"Grandma, Grandma,
are those your cabbages?"

GOOKERS

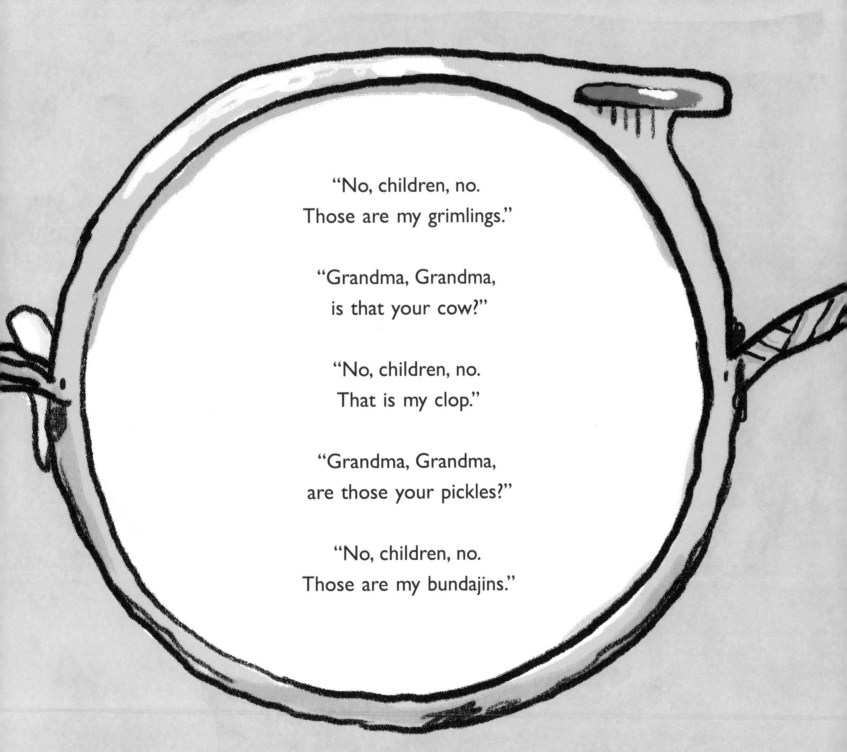

"No, children, no.
Those are my grimlings."

"Grandma, Grandma,
is that your cow?"

"No, children, no.
That is my clop."

"Grandma, Grandma,
are those your pickles?"

"No, children, no.
Those are my bundajins."

"Grandma, Grandma,
put on your goggly gookers.
The clop is in the fizz-bustle
eating all the grimlings.
If you don't get her out
you'll be in a bundajin.
And that's a fact!"

THE LITTLE TRACTOR

Once, on the edge of town, there was a beautiful farm with a nice little tractor and a boy with sticky-up hair.

But the boy grew up, the tractor grew old, and the town swallowed the farm.

After many years in a tumbledown shed, the tractor was put in a car sales yard, where it sat with grass seeds on its engine and dreams of sweet earth on its old tyres.

The salesman said to his customers:

It's a nice little tractor, a strong little tractor, a chug-chug, can't-go-wrong little tractor.

"Bless my barnacles! I'll buy it!" said the man with a salty smile. "This tractor will do for my boat."

So, every day, the tractor pulled a boat to the sea and backed it into the water.

But the tractor did not like sitting in the sloppy, salty sea with seagulls on its hood. Its engine rumbled and grumbled, and it stopped.

Back to the car sales yard it went, back to the salesman, who cried:

**It's a nice little tractor, a strong little tractor,
a chug-chug, can't-go-wrong little tractor.**

"Well, hacketty-hack and chippetty-chop!" said a woman with sawdust in her pockets. "Just what I want for my firewood business."

So, every day, the tractor pulled a trailer heaped with firewood around the city houses.

But this was no job for a tractor with grass seeds on its engine and dreams of sweet earth on its tyres.

Its pistons flapped, its oil boiled, and it stopped.

Once again, the tractor went back to the car sales yard and the salesman, who said:

**It's a nice little tractor, a strong little tractor,
a chug-chug, can't-go-wrong little tractor.**

"Jingle bells!" cried a man with a beard. "The tractor will pull the Santa float in the downtown Christmas parade."

The tractor did its best…but the Santa float was huge and the street was very steep.

The gears slipped, the wheels flipped, and the Santa float ran back into the sugar plum fairies.

Once more, the little tractor was returned to the car sales yard. This time, the salesman did not say it was a nice little tractor, a strong little tractor, a chug-chug, can't-go-wrong little tractor.

He didn't say anything.

The tractor sat and sat.

One wild spring day, along came a man with sticky-up hair, grass seeds on his shirt and sweet earth on his boots.

"What's a nice little tractor like you doing in a car sales yard?" he said.

Then the man looked closer.

"I don't believe it!" he cried, and he hugged the little tractor with such big, huggly hugs that everyone stared.

The man with the sticky-up hair bought the nice little tractor and drove it to his beautiful farm far from town.

There to meet him were his wife and five handsome children, all with sticky-up hair.

The man cried, "I found the tractor we had way back when I was a boy."

**It's a nice little tractor, a strong little tractor,
a chug-chug, can't-go-wrong little tractor.**

The little tractor hummed and purred.
Did it go wrong?
Of course it didn't. It chug-chugged happily ever after.

SUPER JUMBLE

There was trouble in the jungle
when a buffalo tried to swingle
like a monkey from a bundle of vines.

He got into a tangle
and was left there to dangle
at a very awkward angle, in the lines.

The animals came to goggle
and giggle at the bungle
while the buffalo gave a wriggle to get free.

But not a wiggle or a jiggle
could help him in his struggle
as he dangled in a tangle from the tree.

The buffalo thought he'd strangle
and panic made him tingle
and he gave a loud gurgle of despair.

But high about the jungle
with a jingle and a spangle,
flew the great SuperJumble through the air.

Now, the elephant SuperJumble,
though really very humble,
was the strongest and most nimble on the earth.

When animals were in trouble
she would fly there at the double,
her bright-red cloak awaggle round her girth.

As the buffalo in a tangle
wriggled vainly at an angle
and cried out in a gargle of fear,

beneath him in the jungle
came a warm and friendly rumble.
"Do not struggle! SuperJumble is here."

Then without fuss or fumble
she flew into the tangle
and freed him with a single trunk blow.

The buffalo thought he'd tumble
but she took him like a bundle
to the bottom of the jungle below.

The buffalo was agoggle.
He had no chance to babble,
for away went SuperJumble in the air.

But the next time there is trouble
she'll be back at the double.
You can count on SuperJumble to be there.

DO NOT
DROP YOUR
JELLYBEANS

Please, do not drop your jellybeans.

If you drop your jellybeans,
the baby will wake up and cry like a fire alarm.

If the baby cries like a fire alarm,
the firefighters will come to the house.

They will turn on their big whooshing hoses.

You could get washed away in the flood.

You might even end up in the river.

If you end up in the river,
you could drift out to the wild salt sea.

You could be attacked by sharks and giant squid.

A pirate ship might chase you.

You and the ship might be caught in a huge storm.

Oh, the lightning!

Oh, the thunder!
Oh, the waves!

The pirate ship could be wrecked on some rocks
but you could be saved by a humpback whale.

The whale could take you all the way to the Arctic Ocean.

Then, before you could say a word,
the whale might leave you on an iceberg.

You are not dressed for icebergs.

So, please, please, please, do not drop your jellybeans.

Uh-oh! You did it!

You
dropped
your
jellybeans!

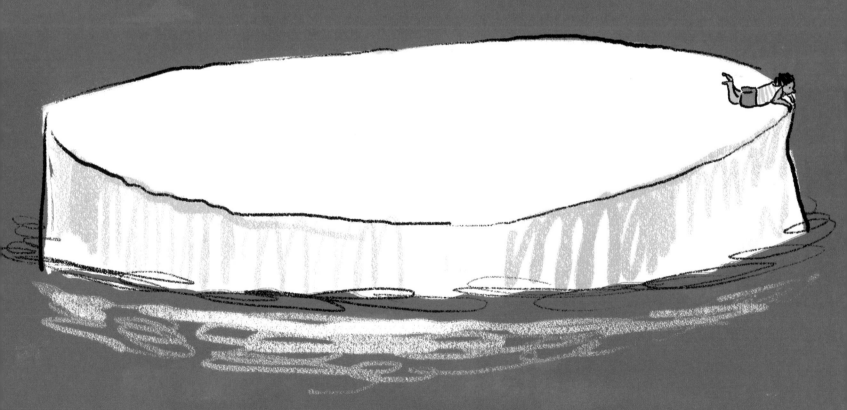

CHEESE TRAP

Once upon a mousetime,
two little squeaks went cheesing…
searching for cheese, strong yellow cheese,
cheese as round as the moon.

Under the kitchen table,
the old grey meow was sleeping.
With snorting snores and twitching claws,
she dreamed of squeaky mice.

Quickly up the table leg,
the little squeaks went sneaking.
Then—sniff, sniff—they caught a whiff
of cheese in a great glass dish.

They tried to lift the lid off…
the glass was far too heavy.
But their huffs and puffs were loud enough
to waken the sleeping meow.

The old grey meow came out with a yowl
and the two little squeaks went running…
down the table, across the floor
and under the kitchen door.

Now the old grey meow was far too stiff
for kittenish leaping and pouncing,
but that wise cat knew a thing or two
and she planned to catch those mice.

Back on the floor by the table,
the old meow lay like a statue,
her mouth open wide, with the cheese inside,
waiting for the squeaks to return.

As she waited with baited breath,
the squeaks sneaked back to the kitchen.
They could smell the cheese strong on the breeze,
and it made their whiskers shake.

As quietly as two little feathers,
the squeaks came closer and closer...
paw after paw, towards the cat's jaw
and the marvellous mound of cheese.

A-a-a-a-a-chooo!

And she blew it!

She really blew it!

The cheese...

the squeaks...

her supper...

She blew them right away.

Back inside their mousehole,
the squeaks were ready for feasting.
They nibbled…

and spat!

"We can't eat that!

It smells like
the old grey cat!"

THE CIRCUS

The elephants went to the circus
to see the people perform.
They had bags of peanuts and popcorn,
and mufflers to keep them warm.

The acrobats and the jugglers
made them trumpet with delight,
but when the tightrope walker slipped,
they turned pale grey with fright.

They liked the daring trapeze act
and gave a big cheer for the clown,
who ran around the circus ring
with his britches falling down.

But one young elephant did not cheer.
In fact she looked quite sad.
"Why do we make these people perform?"
she asked her elephant dad.

"They enjoy it, dear," her father said.
"They have good food for wages.
And every night they get to sleep
in clean and comfortable cages.

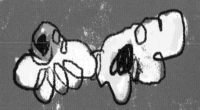

"Just think how very fortunate
these people are, my child.
They're better fed and safer
than the humans in the wild."

NOBODY KNOWS

Nobody knows, nobody knows
how the elephant blows his nose.
Does he go Choo! in a paper tissue?
Or does he sniff in a handkerchief?
Or does he wipe it on his toes?
How does the elephant blow his nose?

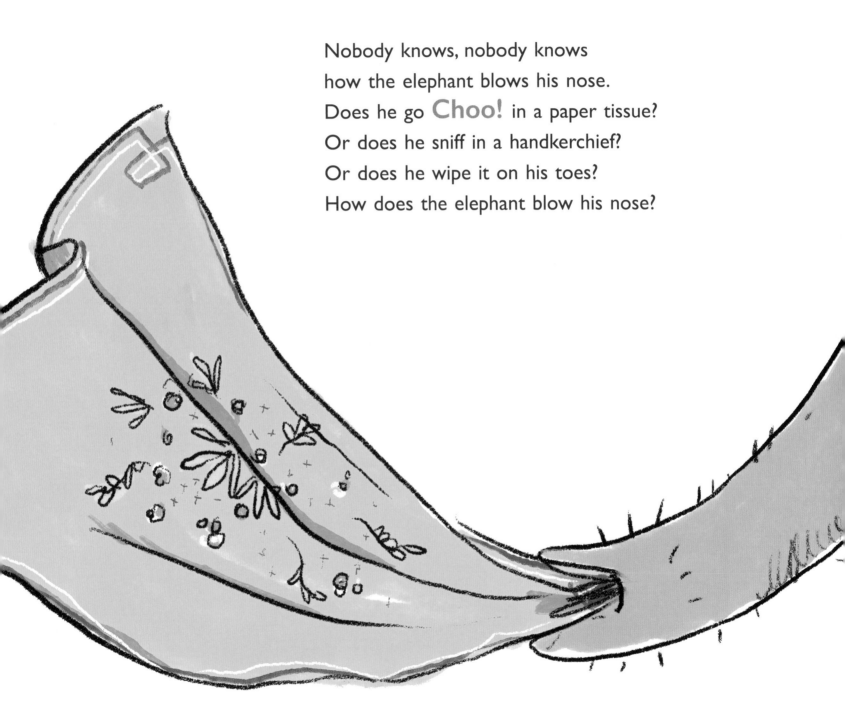

UNCLE ANDY'S SINGLET

Uncle Andy bought the singlet
from an army surplus store.
It was the only upper garment
Uncle Andy ever wore.

It kept him warm on winter nights
and cool in summer heat,
a singlet that was long enough
to dry his muddy feet.

"Oh, I will sing of the singlet,"
cried our Uncle Andy.
"A good old cotton singlet
will always come in handy."

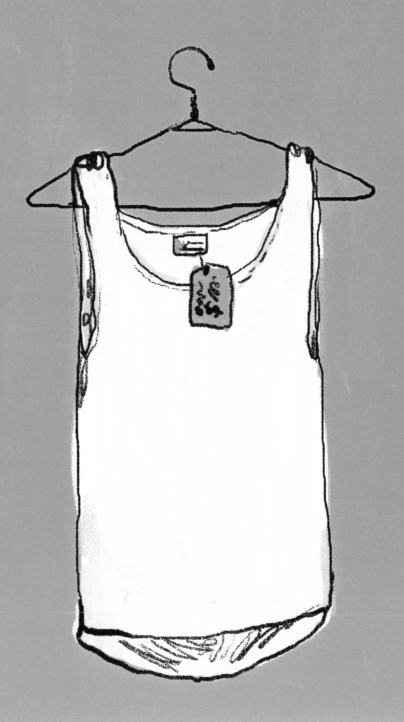

The singlet made a useful pouch
to carry new-laid eggs
or veggies from the garden
or fresh-killed mutton legs.

Once it tied a gate up
when Andy had no wire.
It wrapped a leaking water pipe.
It beat a bracken fire.

"Oh, I will sing of the singlet,"
cried our Uncle Andy.
"A good old cotton singlet
will always come in handy."

When Andy went out fishing,
he took it off his back,
tied a knot in one end,
and made a herring sack.

At home, he had a fry-up
of little silver fishes,
and then he used the singlet
to dry his breakfast dishes.

"Oh, I will sing of the singlet,"
our Uncle Andy cries.
"There's only one small problem—
it does attract the flies!"

FASTER

Billy Castor had been a pirate, but now he had a job driving a bus. He still wore his pirate clothes.

He had a green jacket and gold earrings and a black hat with a yellow feather in it. The feather was for good luck.

Every morning, Billy Castor put on his hat and sang, "Day and night, night and day, my feather keeps bad luck away."

As he got on his bus, he sang, "Never, never, no not ever, will I drive without my feather."

FASTER

But one day, a strong wind tugged Billy Castor's feather out of his hat, and it flew away like a yellow arrow.

"Gone!" cried Billy Castor.

"Gone!" cried all the passengers.

Billy Castor sat on the step of his bus and moaned deep moans.

"Time to go," said the passengers.

"No, no, I cannot go!" Billy Castor replied. "Without my lucky feather, I will have a dreadful accident."

"But we'll be late!" said the passengers.

"Better to be late than dead on time," said Billy Castor.

One of the men said, "Listen, Mr Castor. Perhaps I can help. In my pet shop there's a yellow parrot. I can't let you pull out a feather, but I can sell you the whole bird."

"A whole yellow parrot!" laughed Billy Castor. "Just think! All that luck sitting on my hat!"

"There is one problem," said the man. "To get the parrot, you must drive your bus to my pet shop."

Billy Castor stopped laughing. As he climbed into his seat, he shook from toes to teeth. How could he drive without a good-luck feather?

"Accident!" he groaned as he started the engine.

"Accident!" he moaned all the way down the road.

But he didn't have an accident. He drove very well. He stopped the bus by the pet shop. The man got out and came back with a yellow parrot. Sure enough, the parrot was covered from head to tail with good-luck feathers.

"This bird is used to traffic," said the man. "It once belonged to a racing driver. Here you are. Good luck!"

"Thank you, my friend! Thank you!" cried Billy Castor, giving him a gold coin.

The parrot hopped on the bus and looked around with a wicked eye. "Okay, okay," it said. "Let's get this show on the road."

Billy Castor drove his bus into the morning traffic. He was no longer afraid. The parrot had thousands of feathers and they would all bring good luck.

The bird hopped up and down on his hat.

"Get moving!"

it screeched.

"We are moving," said Billy Castor.

"You could have fooled me!" said the parrot. "Come on! Put your foot down!"

The bus went faster but not fast enough. The parrot had belonged to a racing driver. It hungered for speed. It thirsted for speed.

"Give it the gas!" the parrot cried.

Billy Castor went as fast as he could. Shops rushed past. The bus rocked from side to side and cars honked in alarm.

"Slow down!" yelled the passengers. "You'll have an accident!"

"Don't worry," called Billy Castor. With all those good-luck feathers, he knew he was safe.

The parrot hopped onto his jacket.

"Faster!"

it screamed in his ear.

It swung on his gold earring.

"Faster, faster, Billy Castor!"

The bus rocked over the hill and down the other side.

It went so fast that the wheels left the road.

"Stop!" yelled the passengers.

Billy Castor could not stop. He had lost control of the bus. It raced down the hill and into the park.

It bounced over a football field. It splashed through a duck pond. Then it stopped in the middle of a flower garden.

The parrot lay on the floor in a tangle of yellow feathers.

"Disaster, Billy Castor!"

it screeched.

The passengers got out. "We'll walk the rest of the way," they said.

The parrot followed them. "Call yourself a driver!" it screeched at Billy Castor. "Look what you've done! I don't need you. I'm off to find a racing driver."

Billy Castor yelled back, "Call yourself a good-luck parrot! I don't need you, either. I don't even need one of your feathers. I can drive better on my own!"

He backed the bus away from the garden, promising to come back and fix up the flowers. Then he drove out of the park. His toes did not shake. His teeth did not shiver.

He didn't moan or groan.

"A good driver doesn't need good luck," he said to himself.

Along the road, he stopped for more passengers. As they got on the bus, he sang in a cheerful voice, "Never, never, no not ever, will I need another feather."

Then down the road he went, saying to himself, "That feather was a lot of nonsense! Nothing but silly superstition!"

But he kept his fingers crossed on the steering wheel, just to make sure.

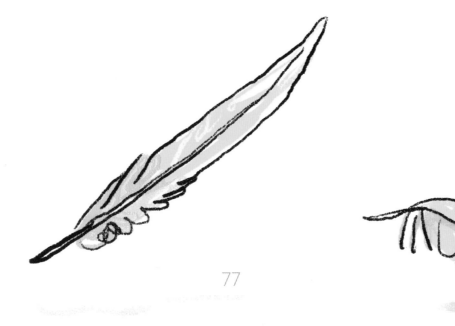

THE JUMBAROO

At the Washington Zoo
the Jumbaroo
got a pain in its woggly.

Woggly woggly
Jumbaroo.

The pain got worse.
It called for the nurse.
"I think I've got the flue-flam!"

Flue-flam flue-flam
woggly woggly
Jumbaroo.

Then its woggly got
some dark blue spots,
and the nurse said,
"It's the bleezles!"

Bleezles bleezles
flue-flam flue-flam
woggly woggly
Jumbaroo.

"I do feel blue,"
said the Jumbaroo.
"By morning I'll be drodbeat."

Drodbeat drodbeat
bleezles bleezles
flue-flam flue-flam
woggly woggly
Jumbaroo.

"Lift up your head,"
the good nurse said,
"And I'll give you a dose of
slushus."

Slushus slushus
drodbeat drodbeat
bleezles bleezles
flue-flam flue-flam
woggly woggly
Jumbaroo.

The Jumbaroo said, "Hey!
The pain's gone away!
And the dark blue spots are vanshoo!"

Vanshoo vanshoo
slushus slushus
drodbeat drodbeat
bleezles bleezles
flue-flam flue-flam
woggly woggly
Jumbaroo.

Now if you too,
are like the Jumbaroo
with dark blue spots on your woggly,
have a luscious
dose of slushus
and you'll be right as goggly.

Goggly goggly
vanshoo vanshoo
slushus slushus
drodbeat drodbeat
bleezles bleezles
flue-flam flue-flam
woggly woggly
Jumbaroo.
Jumbaroo! Hey!

GREEDY

Mum went shopping
and got some sausages.
Along came Greedy Cat.
He looked in the shopping bag.

**Gobble
gobble
gobble**

and that was the end of that.

Mum went shopping
and got some sticky buns.
Along came Greedy Cat.
He looked in the shopping bag.

**Gobble
gobble
gobble**

and that was the end of that.

Mum went shopping
and got some potato chips.
Along came Greedy Cat.
He looked in the shopping bag.

Gobble
gobble
gobble

and that was the end of that.

Mum went shopping
and got some bananas.
Along came Greedy Cat.
He looked in the shopping bag.

Gobble
gobble
gobble

and that was the end of that.

Mum went shopping
and got some chocolate.
Along came Greedy Cat.
He looked in the shopping bag.

**Gobble
gobble
gobble**

and that was the end of that.

Mum went shopping
and got a pot of pepper.
Along came Greedy Cat.
He looked in the shopping bag.

**Gobble
gobble—**

YOW!

And that was the end of that!

"In all the stories I write,
Small is the winner. Small is powerful.
Big may not solve problems for Small,
but Small may solve problems for Big.
Small always wins. The story loves Small."

JOY COWLEY is a much-celebrated New Zealand children's
writer who has won a multitude of awards and honours, including
the Prime Minister's Award for contribution to literature 2010.
In 2018 she was made a Member of the Order of New Zealand
and shortlisted for the Hans Christian Andersen Award.